The Mask of Power

Eruptor
Meets the
Nightmare King

GROSSET & DUNLAP
Penguin Young Readers Group
An Imprint of Penguin Random House LLC

Written by Cavan Scott
Illustrated by Dani Geremia—Beehive Agency

ISBN 978-1-101-99604-1   10 9 8 7 6 5 4 3 2 1

The Mask of Power

Eruptor
Meets the
Nightmare King

by Onk Beakman

Grosset & Dunlap
An Imprint of Penguin Random House

About the Author

Onk Beakman knew he wanted to be a world-famous author from the moment he was hatched. In fact, the book-loving penguin was so excited that he wrote his first novel while still inside his egg (to this day, nobody is entirely sure where he got the tiny pencil and notebook from).

Growing up on the icy wastes of Skylands' Frozen Desert was difficult for a penguin who hated the cold. While his brothers plunged into the freezing waters, Onk could be found with his beak buried in a book and a pen clutched in his flippers.

Yet his life changed forever when a giant floating head appeared in the skies above the tundra. It was Kaos, attempting to melt the icecaps so he could get his grubby little hands on an ancient weapon buried beneath the snow.

Onk watched open-beaked as Spyro swept in and sent the evil Portal Master packing. From that day, Onk knew that he must chronicle the Skylanders' greatest adventures. He traveled the length and breadth of Skylands, collecting every tale he could find about Master Eon's brave champions.

Today, Onk writes from a shack on the beautiful sands of Blistering Beach with his two pet sea cucumbers.

Chapter One

The Frozen Seas

Anyone who has ever traveled to Skylands knows that it's a magical place. It's made up of an infinite number of floating realms; there's an island for everyone. Do you like sun-drenched golden sands? No problem—head to Blistering Beach. Prefer the dark? Then you'll love Moonlight Mountains. There's even an island where volcanoes spew sweet popcorn high into the sky. Perfect if you're feeling a little hungry.

Of course, not every island is popular. Take the Frozen Seas, for example. As the name suggests, it's a chilly, unforgiving place.

Massive waves of ice hang in the air, frozen in place since an everlasting winter fell upon the island millions of years ago. It's so cold that visitors eat ice cream to warm themselves up!

Only people who really, really like the cold go to the Frozen Seas—which is why a Skylander by the name of Eruptor started this adventure in a particularly bad mood.

Eruptor is a lava monster, born in the bowels of a volcano. The kind that gushes red-hot magma, not popcorn. He's hotheaded in every sense of the word. Scalding lava

bubbles beneath his rocky skin, ready to erupt at any moment, and he has a temper to match. Most of the time he keeps his bad moods in check, but he can't help boiling over every now and then. Such as when he's cold, for example. And on this day he was very, very cold.

Eruptor gritted his teeth as he appeared on the top of one of those gigantic frozen waves. The wind had cut through him as soon as he leaped from a Portal, chilling him to his molten core.

"N-not g-good," he stuttered, teeth chattering like castanets. "N-not g-good at-t-t all!"

"What are you talking about, Eruptor?" said the hulking four-armed creature who appeared beside him. "This looks cool to me!"

"That's the problem," snarled Eruptor, turning to face the newcomer. "It's all right for you, Slam Bam. You take an ice bath every night!"

It was true. As a yeti, Slam Bam loved subzero conditions. In fact, before he became a Skylander, he had lived on a floating glacier. He'd spent his days carving ice sculptures and eating snow cones. His arctic existence only came to an end when an evil Portal Master known as Kaos blasted Slam Bam's glacier, sending him adrift. Luckily, the yeti washed up on an island that belonged to Master Eon, the greatest Portal Master of them all.

Master Eon had invited Slam Bam to join the Skylanders, the brave band of heroes who protect Skylands from villains like Kaos and his menacing minions. That is how Slam Bam had met Eruptor. Despite their differing temperatures, the two Skylanders became firm friends, united in their fight against the forces of The Darkness.

Slam Bam had always wanted to visit the Frozen Seas, but had never managed to persuade Eruptor to join him—until today. Master Eon had received a cry for help from the Frozen Seas' icy wastes and quickly dispatched the two heroes to investigate, along with a third Skylander.

"It's fright time!" Grim Creeper said as he appeared through the Portal, swirling his super-sharp scythe in excitement.

"Hey, watch what you're doing, Grim." Slam Bam chuckled, raising two of his arms in fake alarm. "I don't need a haircut right now."

Grim Creeper grinned. "Sorry, Slam. I'm just excited to be here."

Master Eon came across Grim Creeper

after the young ghost saved the prestigious Grim Acres School for Ghost Wrangling. At first, Grim had been turned away from the academy. The Scaremaster in charge thought that the young spirit didn't have what it took to be a reaper. Then Grim Acres was attacked by a gang of galloping ghouls. The other pupils turned and fled in terror, but Grim Creeper stood his ground, saving students and teachers alike from the pesky poltergeists. Grim Creeper was welcomed into the school and, after he graduated, went on to join the Skylanders. This was his first mission, and the Undead Skylander was itching to get started.

"So, what do we do now?" Grim Creeper asked.

"Go home?" Eruptor grumbled.

A look of shock passed over the phantom's face. "You're kidding, right?"

"Of course he is." Slam Bam laughed. "Eruptor never gives up, no matter how much he moans. Ain't that right?" The yeti nudged Eruptor in the ribs, causing the hair on his elbows to sizzle slightly against the lava monster's red-hot skin.

Eruptor couldn't hide a sneaky smile. "Cool it, Slam. I've got a rep to protect!"

Before Slam could reply, a scream sounded across the icy ocean.

"HEEEEEEELP!"

"Sounds like someone's in trouble," Grim Creeper said, clutching his scythe tighter than ever.

"That's why we're here," rumbled Eruptor, peering over the edge of the huge wave. "But how do we get down?"

"We slide!" Slam Bam whooped, throwing himself forward. Grim Creeper's eyes widened as he watched the yeti zoom down the near-vertical drop of the frozen wave, arms outstretched like a surfer.

"That looks like fun," the Undead Skylander said, taking off after Slam Bam. "Come on!"

Eruptor shrugged and leaped into action behind the other two Skylanders. The ice beneath his feet hissed as he picked up speed.

"Last one to the bottom's an icicle!" he shouted as he steamed past his friends.

Chapter Two

Cyclops Attack

Eruptor skidded to a halt at the bottom of the wave, throwing up a thick flurry of snow.

"Okay," he said, grinning wildly as Slam Bam appeared at his side. "I admit it. That was pretty cool."

"Nice sliding, bro," Slam Bam said, fist-pumping the lava monster. "You're a real natural!"

"I've always told you I'm hot stuff!" Eruptor quipped, before turning his attention to the frozen landscape in front of them. "Now, who needs our help?"

As if in answer, another terrified scream echoed across the ice:

"HELP US!"

"This way," Grim Creeper cried as he slid straight past the others and started scurrying toward a campsite in the distance.

As the Skylanders drew closer, it became obvious what danger awaited them. Small figures scampered between the huts and tents, waving sharp spears and heavy shovels.

Eruptor's mouth curled into a snarl. "Cyclopses," he growled. "Those one-eyed weirdos make my blood boil!"

"Don't worry," replied Slam Bam, his hands already curled into fists. "They're about to face a cold snap!"

"Yeah," agreed Grim Creeper. "Let's give them the fright of their lives!"

On the edge of the camp, a cyclops saw something out of the corner of his only eye. He turned and let out a tiny squeak of terror. You see, cyclopses are basically cowardly bullies, happy to rampage as long as no one rampages back at them. The campsite that the cyclopses were attacking belonged to a bunch of Treeman archaeologists, thoughtful walking twigs who wouldn't know one end of a rampage from the other. Attacking them was easy. They just rolled over and gave up.

Skylanders were different, though. Skylanders were powerful. Skylanders were brave.

Skylanders never gave up.

Panicking, the cyclops raised his spear in the air and yelled, "Incoming!"

All around him, his fellow cyclopses stopped terrorizing Treemen and turned to face the advancing Skylanders. Almost as one, the cyclopses swallowed hard and readied their defenses. A row of Cyclops Snowblasters appeared in the snow, letting loose a barrage of snowballs. At the same time, Cyclops Sleet-Throwers loaded snow and ice on to their shovels and started chucking it at the heroes.

Nearing the campsite, Slam Bam raised all four of his hands and a wall of ice magically appeared between the Skylanders and the cyclopses. The Snowblasters' snowballs impacted harmlessly against the icy shield, giving Eruptor the chance he needed.

"Fire!" he yelled, shooting balls of liquid lava into the air. They dropped into the ice behind the Snowblasters, sending steam shooting into the air. In seconds, the campsite was shrouded in scalding mist.

"Spooktacular!" Grim Creeper laughed and sent his spectral scythe spinning past Slam Bam's ice blocks. The weapon slammed into the Snowblasters one by one as the Skylanders rushed into the fray.

At the center of the battle, Bloodshot the Cyclops Gazermage peered through his massive magical magnifying glass.

Through the fog, the one-eyed wizard could see his forces being attacked and hear the sound of whistling scythes, thumping fists, and flaming lava blobs.

This was why he'd never wanted to command a cyclops squadron in the first place. He'd been far happier studying magical scrolls back at the Crystal Eye Castle. But, like all minions of evil, Bloodshot knew that when his master called he couldn't disobey.

And who was his master? Bloodshot waved a hand over his magnifying glass. The lens flared with unnatural light before a face appeared in the center of the bronze hoop. A face that was feared across Skylands. A face that glared back at Bloodshot with blazing red eyes. The face of Kaos!

"Bloodshot!" the evil Portal Master snapped, his voice echoing from the magnifying glass. "What did I tell you?"

Bloodshot shuffled his feet. "Um, not to disturb you until we've found the treasure?"

"Exactly!" Kaos said. "And have you found the treasure?"

Bloodshot's head dropped. "No, sir. We have not."

"THEN WHY DO YOU DARE DISTURB ME, FOOL?" Kaos ranted. "Don't you know it's my day for rearranging my evil potion collection? You know how I hate to be interrupted when I'm rearranging my evil potion collection. Have you forgotten what happened to the last person who interrupted me when I was rearranging my evil potion collection?"

Bloodshot whimpered. How could anyone forget? The last person to interrupt Lord Kaos while he was rearranging his evil potion collection was a Troll by the name of General Monkeywrench. Kaos transformed him into a giant pair of underpants, which he then gave to an underpants-eating rag monster as a light snack. Up to that point, no one had even known that such beasts existed, let alone that they were so partial to undergarments. Needless to say, Bloodshot didn't want to end up going the same way as Monkeywrench—but this was an emergency.

"I—I'm sorry, Lord Kaos," Bloodshot stammered. "But look . . ."

The Gazermage twisted the magnifying glass to show the silhouettes of a certain lava monster, yeti, and reaper.

"SKYLOSERS!" raged Kaos through the lens. "What are they doing there?"

"I think they aim to foil your fiendish plans, my lord!"

"Typical," hissed Kaos. "Anyone would think they don't want me to take over Skylands and spread evil as far as the eye can see."

"I—I know," agreed Bloodshot sheepishly. "It's unbelievable. But what do you want us to do?"

"What do I want you to do?" Kaos shrieked, not believing what his evil little ears were hearing. "I want you to defeat them, you one-eyed NINCOMPOOP! What do you think I want you to do to them?"

Bloodshot's shoulders sagged. He'd hoped that Lord Kaos was going to say that he wanted them to run away as fast as their stubby little legs could carry them. "Oh, okay, then. We'll defeat them. Just checking, you know."

"Then what are you waiting for?" Kaos screeched. "Or do you want me to reach for my Turn Spineless Fools into a Really Big Pair of Bloomers potion? I know it's here somewhere. After all, I was rearranging my evil potions before SOMEONE DISTURBED ME!"

"Y-yes, of couse, Lord Kaos," Bloodshot stammered. "I mean, no, Lord Kaos. We'll get right on it!"

"THEN GET ON WITH IT!" yelled the Portal Master.

Bloodshot didn't hang around any longer. He raised his magnifying glass high in the air and shouted, "CYCLOPS ATTACK!" at the top of his voice—which, to be honest, wasn't a very high place.

It didn't matter anyway. While Bloodshot had been talking to his dark master, the Skylanders had waded through the Coldspear Cyclopses, the Sleet-Throwers, and even the Snowblasters. Bloodshot's troops were lying on the ice, single eyes spinning. And the Skylanders? They were standing around Bloodshot in a rather menacing ring.

"Now, what have we here?" asked Eruptor, looking the trembling cyclops up and down.

"I don't know," replied Slam Bam, watching as the Gazermage peered at them through his oversize magnifying glass, "but it's plain to see that it's no good hiding behind that thing!"

"O-oh yeah?" stammered Bloodshot, not feeling half as brave as he was trying to sound. "Well, here's one in the eye for you!"

A beam of dazzling light burst from the lens and hit Eruptor full-on.

Chapter Three

A Chilling Discovery

Eruptor was thrown back by the blast, cutting a deep trail through the ice.

The other Skylanders quickly retaliated, with Grim Creeper swiping through the air with his scythe. Bloodshot ducked, the blade neatly slicing off the top of his pointed hat. But he found it impossible to evade the ice prison that Slam Bam created around him.

"That's put him on ice," the yeti rumbled as Eruptor got back to his feet. "You okay, Eruptor?"

"Of course I am," the lava monster shot back. "It'll take more than a little squirt like that to make me hot under the collar."

The Skylanders turned as a weedy voice called over to them. "Oh, thank the benevolent ancients that you've arrived," it said. "I thought we were done for."

A thin Treeman with a bushy mustache stomped over. Cumbersome snowshoes were attached to his narrow feet.

"Don't worry," said Slam Bam, holding out a hand. "You're safe now."

"Dead safe," added Grim Creeper.

The Treeman cautiously took Slam Bam's massive paw, obviously hoping that the muscular yeti wouldn't shake his hand too vigorously. "Indeed we are, Skylanders. Thanks to you. My name is Professor Splinters. I am the leader of this expedition."

Eruptor made the introductions on behalf of the group. "Well, I'm Eruptor. My four-armed friend is Slam Bam, and this is Grim Creeper."

Professor Splinters nodded nervously. "Yes, we . . . um . . . we know who you are. In fact, we were about to call you before the cyclopses attacked."

"You were?" Eruptor said, his boiling brow creasing. "Why?"

The Treeman wrung his gnarled hands together. "I think it's better that I show— YAAAARGH!" Professor Splinters screamed as one of his wooden arms caught alight. Eruptor turned to see that Bloodshot had melted his way out of Slam Bam's ice prison and was turning his fire on the weakest member of the group.

"Typical bully," the lava monster roared, opening his mouth wide. "Makes me sick!"

One of Eruptor's less polite habits is belching out streams of lava. It can happen when he's nervous, surprised, angry, or just plain bored. On this occasion it was aimed right at the Gazermage. Bloodshot turned to flee, but it was too late. The flowing magma cut a deep crevice in the ice beneath the cyclops's feet.

"Lord Kaos, help me!" Bloodshot squealed as he fell, his cry breaking off with a loud *crunch*.

The Skylanders peered into the crevice. The dazed cyclops had landed on a glittering heap of jewels and coins.

"Whoa, shiny!" Slam Bam exclaimed.

"Good heavens!" exclaimed Professor Splinters, cradling his charred arm. "You've uncovered buried treasure, Eruptor."

"He has?" said Bloodshot, looking around the bottom of the pit. With a burst of hysterical laughter, the Gazermage scrabbled through the treasure until he snatched up a tiny golden coin.

"Ha-ha-ha-ha-haaaaa!" he cackled uncontrollably. "I've found it! Lord Kaos, I've found it!"

"Found what?" Grim Creeper asked as the cyclops hopped from one foot to the other in excitement.

"Trouble!" Eruptor warned as dark clouds started to roll across the normally clear sky.

"Well done, Bloodshot," said a booming voice. "You're not as foolish as you look!"

The clouds parted to reveal a gigantic glowing head leering down at the Skylanders.

"Kaos!" Slam Bam hissed.

"Come to fight us yourself, huh?" jeered Eruptor.

"That's the spirit," called Grim Creeper.

"Fight you?" the floating head said with a snort. "Why would I waste my time, SKYBLUNDERERS?"

"Good point," Grim Creeper yelled back, undaunted by the eerie lightning that flashed through the black clouds. "Your time is up, and everyone knows it."

"My time is up?" barked Kaos. "I don't think so, DIM CREEPER! Now, that I have that coin, I have all the time in the world! The age of the Skylanders is over. Now is the age of KAOOOOOS!"

Before the Skylanders could respond, the floating head exploded into a blaze of light. Eruptor threw up a hand to protect his eyes, but when the glare subsided Kaos was gone—as was the Gazermage at the bottom of the pit.

"What was that all about?" asked Slam Bam.

Eruptor shook his head. "Beats me. The little creep's making even less sense than usual."

"I think I might have an idea," said Professor Splinters mournfully. "You'd better come with me."

The Skylanders exchanged confused glances as the Treeman led them to the entrance of an underground cave.

"We found this tunnel in the first week of our expedition," Professor Splinters explained. "However, we only uncovered its terrible secret this morning. A chilling discovery, you might say."

Eruptor made a face. "Why don't I like the sound of that?"

Professor Splinters ducked through the low entrance, beckoning for the others to follow.

The tunnel was steep, with a slippery, icy floor. Eruptor went ahead of his two friends, his natural glow lighting a safe path through the gloom.

After trudging deeper and deeper in silence, they found themselves in a huge chamber. A mass of stalactites hung from the roof like dragon's teeth.

"This entire space was filled with ice," the Treeman explained, grabbing a flaming torch from the wall. "We've been clearing it bit by bit, unearthing amazing artifacts from the dawn of Skylands itself."

"Like the coin Kaos was so excited about?" Slam Bam asked, his breath frosting in the chilled air of the cave.

"Bigger than that," Splinters said. "Pottery. Weapons. Even statues."

He swung the torch around to illuminate

a tall and regal sculpture carved from a diamond.

"Whoa!" said Slam Bam as the light of the torch reflected off the statue's sparkling face.

"Whoa indeed, Skylander!" said Splinters, leading them to a wall of ice at the far end of the chamber. "We still have a lot of ice to clear, but there's something else."

"What?" asked Grim Creeper, unable to keep the excitement from his ghostly voice. "More statues?"

"Not exactly," said the Professor, the light from the torch picking out a figure in the ice. A very familiar figure.

Slam Bam gasped. "But that's impossible . . ."

Grim Creeper agreed. "It has to be a trick."

Eruptor didn't say anything at first. He just stared at the frozen face in the icy prison.

It was like looking into a mirror.

"That's me," he said, not believing what his eyes were seeing. "That's me, trapped in the ice!"

Chapter Four

The Nightmare King

"I don't understand," said Grim Creeper, peering at the figure in the ice. "How can that be you?"

"I don't care," replied Eruptor. "I'm getting me outta there!"

Without another word, Eruptor fired some lava straight at the block of ice. Steam filled the cavern, but the ice stubbornly refused to thaw.

"I don't understand," panted Eruptor. "Why won't it melt?"

Slam Bam pressed a palm against the ice and closed his eyes as if communicating with the frozen water. "Because it's magic, bro. Something is keeping this ice frozen."

"So how are we going to get me out?" Eruptor asked, barely keeping his temper in check.

"And how can you be trapped in there anyway," Grim Creeper added, "when you're already standing out here?"

"Time," said a gentle but strong voice from behind them. "It's all a matter of time."

A tall man with a long white beard entered the chamber. His flowing robes swept across the cavern floor as he walked toward the Skylanders, his staff *tap-tap-tapping* against the stone.

"Master Eon!" Eruptor exclaimed. "What are you doing here?"

"I came as soon as I saw what Professor Splinters had found," the Portal Master replied, his face etched with concern.

"What do you mean you saw it?" Grim Creeper asked.

"I witness everything you see, through my Portal of Power," Master Eon replied. "How else do you think I could watch over you in battle?"

"Well, have you seen this?" Eruptor asked, indicating his frozen double. "Is that really me in there?"

Master Eon bowed his head, and the crystal sphere at the top of his staff glowed for a moment. When the Portal Master raised his head again, his expression was more serious than ever. "Yes, Eruptor. That is indeed you, I'm afraid."

"But how?" Slam Bam asked, shrugging all four of his shoulders. "Not even a Skylander can be in two places at once."

"They can if they've traveled through time."

"But I've never time-traveled," Eruptor said, still confused.

"Not yet," the wise Portal Master said, looking at the lava monster sadly. "But you obviously will. At some point in your future you will travel back in time and become trapped in this sheet of ice."

Master Eon turned to the Treeman archaeologist as the Skylanders let his words sink in. "Professor Splinters, how long has this chamber been filled with ice?"

The Treeman rapped against the ice block with a wooden knuckle. "Almost five thousand years," he replied, pushing his glasses back up his twig-like nose. "Give or take the odd century."

"Five thousand years?" Eruptor gasped, staring at his frozen self.

Master Eon nodded. "I feared as much. Professor Splinters, do you have a coin I could examine?"

The Treeman rummaged around in the satchel that hung from his narrow shoulders. "Yes," he said, drawing out a small golden disk. "I have one here."

He passed the coin to Eon.

"Thank you," said the Portal Master, turning it over in his hand. "And have you identified the face on this coin?"

The Treeman shook his head. "I'm afraid not. It's the same person as the statue, but we have no idea who he was. It's a mystery."

"If only that were true," said Master Eon, sorrowfully.

Slam Bam raised his shaggy eyebrows. "You recognize him, Master Eon?"

The Portal Master nodded. "This is King Nefarion, the most terrifying tyrant ever to rule Skylands."

Eruptor took a closer look at the arrogant face on the gold coin. "So, what makes him so special?"

In answer, Eon turned the coin to show them the other side.

The three Skylanders gasped as one.

"The Mask of Power," whispered Grim Creeper in awe.

"The Mask of *what?*" Professor Splinters asked, looking up from the notebook where he had been carefully jotting all of this down.

Eruptor took up the story. "Thousands of years ago, a wicked king had his Spell Punks create a magical mask that would make him all-powerful."

"He was defeated," continued Grim Creeper, "and the mask was broken into eight pieces. One for each Element."

"Kaos has been searching for the fragments," Slam Bam told the Professor. "He has five of them, and we have one. The other two are still lost."

"And let me guess," added Eruptor, meeting Master Eon's gaze. "The wicked king was this guy."

Master Eon nodded and stepped aside to reveal the diamond statue they had all admired earlier. "Nefarion terrorized Skylands for hundreds of years. The

Skylanders of the time were banished, and the Portal Masters were hunted one by one. Had he not been defeated, the Portal Masters would have been wiped off the face of Skylands. During his reign, his subjects knew him by another name—the Nightmare King."

Slam Bam shivered. "Whoa! Is it me, or did it get colder in here?"

"If I'm right," said Master Eon, "this is Nefarion's throne room, buried beneath the ice for ages. Forgotten . . . until it was unearthed by Professor Splinters."

"But that still doesn't explain why Eruptor's buried here, as well," pointed out Slam Bam.

"True," said Master Eon, "but it can be no coincidence that Kaos sent his cyclopses to . . ."

The Portal Master's voice trailed off and his face suddenly grew pale.

"Master Eon?" said Eruptor, rushing forward. "Are you okay?"

"Dizzy," the Portal Master replied, stumbling backward. "I feel so, so dizzy."

The old man fainted; he was only saved from hitting the cold floor by Slam Bam catching him in his powerful arms.

The silver coin slipped from Eon's fingers and clattered against the stone floor. Moving quickly, Grim Creeper scooped it up and stared at its face in disbelief.

"What's wrong, Grim?" asked Eruptor.

The Undead Skylander showed the lava monster the coin. "This!"

Now it was Eruptor's turn to be amazed. The face of King Nefarion was slowly transforming into the grinning image of Kaos!

Chapter Five

All Change

"Now what's happening?" said Eruptor, feeling giddy himself. "Why's Kaos on the coin instead of . . ."

He paused, searching for the name that Eon had mentioned only moments ago. What was it? Nefari-something? How could he have forgotten it already?

"Nefarion," Master Eon muttered weakly, still slumped in Slam Bam's arms.

"Master Eon," the yeti called. "You're awake!"

"Remember the name," was all the Portal Master could say in reply. "Remember

Nefarion. Can you do that?"

"Of course we can," said Eruptor, helping Eon to stand once again. "Nefarion! See?"

"Who?" asked Grim Creeper, looking confused.

"The Nightmare King," Slam Bam prompted. "The one Master Eon told us about. You know, whatshisname."

Grim Creeper shook his head. "Nope, never heard of him!"

Eruptor was starting to lose his cool. "What's wrong with you, Grim?" He pointed to the diamond statue. "Him!"

"You can't blame Grim Creeper," said Master Eon. "Look!"

They all turned to the statue, only to see it begin to blur. The cruel, regal face was shifting, transforming into someone even crueler.

"But that's Kaos," said Eruptor, now completely bewildered. "Wasn't it someone else before?"

"Don't be ridiculous," snapped Professor

Splinters. "It's always been a statue of Emperor Kaos, all hail his terrible name."

"All hail his what?" asked Slam Bam.

"What happened to Nera-whatsit?" Eruptor asked Master Eon.

The Portal Master was leaning heavily on his staff. "I can't remember, and that's the problem. History is being rewritten even as we speak. I can barely recall the name of the Nightmare King myself."

"What wickedness is this?" Professor Splinters said with a snarl. "You don't remember the name of the Nightmare King? It's Kaos, of course! It always has been! Who are you people, and what are you doing here?"

"You don't know us, Professor?" asked Eruptor. "But you called us here!"

"Impossible!" The Treeman spat.

Eruptor realized for the first time that the Professor's clothes had changed. A minute ago Splinters had been wearing a safari suit and pith helmet, but now the archaeologist was decked out in a suit of shining armor. If that wasn't bad enough, his chest plate was emblazoned with the face of Kaos himself!

The Treeman pointed a long curved sword at the Skylanders that Eruptor was sure hadn't been in his hand before. "You are trespassing in Emperor Kaos's Ice Palace. You must be executed immediately!"

Eruptor had no idea what was happening, but he didn't like it. No one threatened the Skylanders and got away with it—especially after they'd only come to help. "Get ready to feel the burn," he growled, a fresh supply of lava already rumbling in the pit of his stomach.

Beside him, Slam Bam and Grim Creeper dropped into defensive positions, ready to hold back the army of Trolls that had somehow appeared from nowhere behind General Splinters.

General? thought Eruptor. *Didn't Splinters used to be a Professor?*

It didn't matter. If it was a battle Splinters wanted, then a battle he would get.

Eruptor opened his mouth, ready to smother them all in a lava bath.

"No!" shouted Master Eon from behind him. The Portal Master slammed his staff on the flagstones beneath their feet, and there was a sound like thunder. The cavern dissolved in a blinding flash and, when the

Skylanders blinked to clear their eyes, they were standing in Master Eon's own fortress, a long, long way from the Frozen Seas.

"That's better." Master Eon took a breath, slowly rising to his full height. "The walls of the citadel will protect us, for now at least."

"What was all that about?" asked Eruptor.

"Yeah, where did all those Trolls come from?" Slam Bam added.

"And what happened to Splinters?" added Grim Creeper. "Why did he go all evil on us?"

Master Eon staggered over to his Portal of Power, still feeling the effects of whatever had just happened. "History is changing—and I think we all know who's behind it."

Muttering a series of magic words, Eon waved a hand over the Portal. Immediately, its surface began to cloud, and an image formed through the mist.

"Behold, the lair of Kaos . . ."

The Skylanders peered at the image of a dank, dreary-looking chamber, complete with numerous statues of Kaos around its walls. Kaos looking triumphant. Kaos looking angry. Kaos looking smug.

"I don't like what he's done with the place," commented Eruptor. "Where is he?"

"He has gone," Master Eon said sadly.

"Where?"

"Into the past. Look."

Another wave of Eon's hand, and two figures appeared in the room: Kaos and, beside him, his faithful Troll butler, Glumshanks. The evil Portal Master snapped his fingers and, in a flash of light, a Cyclops Gazermage appeared— Bloodshot!

"These are events that have already happened," Master Eon said.

"That's the dude from the dig," Slam Bam pointed out as Bloodshot handed Kaos the coin he'd found in the bottom of the crevice. The Portal Master danced a

little jig—a particularly evil little jig.

"This is it, Glumshanks," they heard Kaos crow. "The moment that I, KAOS, have been waiting for. The day I wipe Eon and his miserable band of Skylanders from history."

"What does he mean?" asked Eruptor, only to be shushed by Master Eon. The elderly Portal Master was staring intently at the scene playing out in front of them.

"Are you ready, Glumshanks?" Kaos asked, "Are you ready to rebuild Skylands in my image?"

"Well, I haven't done the laundry, Lord Kaos," admitted the green Troll. "Your socks haven't been washed for a decade or two."

"My socks can wait, FOOL! Where we are going, I will have as many new socks as I want. Truly evil socks. Socks carved from pure GOLD!"

"Won't that be awfully uncomfortable, Lord—?"

"SILENCE!" Kaos held out his hand.

"Give me the ancient mystical words NOW!"

"The ancient mystical *what*?" asked Glumshanks, exchanging a confused look with Bloodshot.

"The ancient mystical words that will allow us to travel back to the time of the Nightmare King. The ancient mystical words I gave you for safekeeping. The ancient mystical words that you pledged your life to protect, no matter what."

"Oh, those," Glumshanks said, pulling a scrappy piece of parchment from his tattered robes. "Sorry, I thought you meant some other ancient mystical words."

Kaos snatched the paper from the Troll, shooting him his scariest glare. Clearing his throat, the Portal Master held the coin of King Nefarion aloft and began to read aloud.

"One: Wash Lord Kaos's socks.

"Two: Wash Lord Kaos's feet.

"Three: Throw away the cloths I used to wash Lord Kaos's feet.

"Four: Polish Lord Kaos's head . . ."

The Skylanders looked at one another. "They don't sound like ancient mystical words to me," said Grim Creeper.

Kaos seemed to agree. "Glumshanks, what is this?" he shrieked.

The Troll looked sheepish and turned the parchment over in Kaos's hand. "Sorry, Lord Kaos, I must have written my to-do list on the other side. Here."

"When I am all-powerful, remind me to banish you to the Outlands, FOOL!" screamed Kaos.

"Yes, Lord Kaos," replied Glumshanks wearily. "I'll add it to my list."

Kaos returned his attention to the parchment, held the coin back up, and began to read once again:

"*Emit fo sdniw,*
kcab em ekat,
tsap eht ot,
pals a teg ll'uoy ro!"

When nothing happened, Kaos screamed, "These mystical words don't work."

"You could try reading the letters backward, Lord Kaos," Glumshanks suggested.

"I knew that, you FOOL!" Kaos snapped. He began to read the letters backward, then added one final not-so-ancient mystical word: "NOW!"

A rift in the very fabric of time and space appeared behind the Portal Master. Impossible colors twisted inside the hole in the air: reddish-black greens, purplish-orange whites, and sky-bluish pinks. As the Skylanders gaped, Kaos and his butler were sucked through the rift, screaming their heads off, before the hole closed again.

Left alone, Bloodshot blinked in disbelief. "Well, that's something you don't see every day," he muttered to himself.

The surface of the Portal returned to normal.

"Where did they go?" asked Slam Bam.

"Isn't it obvious?" replied Eruptor. "Into the past. Emperor Kaos is going to try to change history."

"All hail his terrible name," muttered Grim Creeper, before slapping a black-gloved hand across his own mouth. "What did I just say?"

"You can't help it," Master Eon said, looking paler than ever. "Emperor Kaos has already conquered the past."

"All hail his terrible name," the three Skylanders said in unison before they could stop themselves. They, too, were being affected by the changes to history.

"He must have gotten fed up with trying to find the segments of the Mask of Power in the present," Eruptor said.

Eon nodded. "He has gone back to take the Mask from King Nefar-whatsit himself."

Outside the Citadel, the light began to dim, gray clouds flooding across the sky.

"He's already won?" asked Slam Bam.

"Never!" said Master Eon. "Grim Creeper, do you still have the coin bearing Emperor Kaos's face?"

"I do," said the reaper, producing the coin and biting his lip so he wouldn't be forced to add *all hail his terrible name.*

"Can you perform the same spell?" asked Eruptor.

"I can," admitted Master Eon. "But powerful words such as these can only be used once by a Portal Master. We can send folk back in time and return them to the present, but that is it."

"So we only have one chance," realized Slam Bam.

"Then we'd better make it count," said Grim Creeper, brandishing his scythe defiantly.

"I'll try to send you back to a point in time before whatshisname steals the Mask of Power," Master Eon explained, turning the coin over in his fingers. "You must stop him from defeating the Nightmare King and creating this future."

"What are we waiting for?" urged Eruptor. "Let's go!"

A worrying thought occurred to Slam Bam. "But, Eruptor, if you head back into the past you'll end up trapped in that ice. We know. We've seen it."

Eruptor avoided his friend's worried gaze. "We have to stop Emperor Kaos—"

"All hail his terrible name!" cut in Slam Bam.

"—whatever it takes!" the lava monster concluded. "Let's put history right!"

He looked up at Master Eon, who smiled at the brave Fire Skylander.

"I knew I could depend on you," the Portal Master said, before raising the coin into the air and reciting the time-travel spell they had heard Kaos say:

"*Winds of time*

take me back
to the past,
or you'll get a slap!"

Behind them, the gateway to the past opened, threatening to drag the Skylanders off their feet.

Eruptor didn't wait. He was the first one to jump through the rift, leaping toward his own destiny.

Chapter Six

The Forest of Fire

"Traveling through a Portal of Power is like the best roller-coaster ride ever. Fun, but a little scary the first time you do it.

Traveling through time turned out to be the complete opposite of fun. Eruptor felt as if he was first being turned inside out and then outside in, before the entire process repeated all over again.

It was like falling down a never-ending tunnel. Or should that be falling *up* a never-ending tunnel? Eruptor found it hard to tell, especially with so many images of Skylands' history flashing past his eyes. He saw the

SWAP Force defending Mount Cloudbreak, followed by the Giants defeating the Arkeyan King. Then there were glimpses of events he knew nothing about. The shriek of a four-headed beast and the blast of a huge explosion. Master Eon's Citadel lying in ruins. The Skylanders flying through space toward a distant blue-and-green planet. No, it had to be his mind playing tricks on him. He couldn't really be seeing the past and the future mixing together . . . could he?

He was spinning faster now, around and around and around. His body felt like it was stretching, like it was a pack of hot dogs caught in a tug of war between two Chompies. He felt as if his body was about to snap in two.

"Can't . . . take . . . much . . . more . . . of . . . this!" he moaned, his voice distorting in the time tunnel.

Suddenly he saw a light up ahead, burning brighter than a million suns. Eruptor tried to turn away from it, but he was being pulled closer and closer and closer, and then . . .

WHUMPH!

Eruptor hit the ground, hard. He didn't mind. In fact, he laughed—a deep, booming belly laugh that made his sides ache. He rolled on to his back and felt warm air on his skin.

He'd made it through the time tunnel. He was alive. But where was he? Eruptor sat up and looked around. A ring of tall, green trees encircled a clearing of lush grass. Insects chirped loudly and birds sung high in the air.

WHUMPH!

Another body hit the ground behind him. Eruptor turned to see Grim Creeper sitting on his own head, his translucent legs pinwheeling in the air.

Another crash to their right delivered Slam Bam, all four of his arms tangled up in a knot of limbs.

"Whoa," groaned the yeti. "That's the last time I'll complain about Flynn's bumpy rides." Grim Creeper flipped over onto his

feet. "Is this the past?" the reaper asked.

"Your guess is as good as mine," said Eruptor.

"But this is a forest," said Slam Bam, untangling his arms. "I thought King Nefarion's castle was in the Frozen Seas?" A smile spread over the yeti's face. "Hey, I remembered the Nightmare King's name!"

Eruptor tried something for himself. "Kaos," he said. "Kaos, Kaos, Kaos, Kaos!" Now the lava monster was grinning, too. "I don't have to call him Emperor Kaos!"

"You don't have to hail his terrible name,

either," pointed out Grim Creeper.

"Master Eon did it!" Slam Bam realized.
"Kaos obviously hasn't got his grubby little
mitts on the Mask of Power yet! We still have
time to save the future!"

Eruptor rubbed his temples. "If you say so.
All of this time traveling is making my brain
hurt."

"I don't know what you're complaining
about," Slam Bam said, fanning himself with
three of his hands. "This place is sweltering.
You must love it."

"I don't know," Eruptor grumbled. "It

could be a little hotter." Behind him, a tree burst into flames. "Me and my big mouth."

"Eruptor!" exclaimed Slam Bam. "Did you do that?"

"No," insisted the lava monster. Fire broke out in the branches of two more trees around the clearing. Then three. Then four! Soon, every single tree was ablaze.

"Well, someone's turning up the heat!" yelled Grim Creeper. Faces were forming in the flickering flames. Angry-looking faces.

"I think it's the trees themselves," Eruptor realized. "They're alive."

"THIS IS THE FOREST OF FIRE!" boomed the first tree that had caught alight. "YOU ARE ENEMIES OF THE NIGHTMARE KING!"

"Actually," said Slam Bam, "we're kind of here to help him. He's in danger from an evil Portal Master from the future. We've come back to stop him!"

"LIAR!" screamed the trees as one.

"I gotta admit, I'm finding it hard to believe myself," admitted Eruptor, but the trees weren't listening. They were pulling back their branches as if they were about to throw something at the Skylanders. Which is exactly what they did.

"Fireballs!" warned Eruptor as the first one fizzed toward the Skylanders. "Defend yourselves!"

"No kidding," Slam Bam shouted back, surrounding them with a wall of ice—not that the barrier would last long.

"Time to cut and run," yelled Grim Creeper, vaulting over a rapidly thawing ice block. He raced across the clearing, waving his scythe above his head.

Eruptor wasn't about to let his spooky friend put himself in danger on his own. He opened his mouth, swallowing an incoming fireball.

"Mmmmm," he said, licking his lips. "Hot and spicy! Just how I like it!"

The lava monster leaped around, gobbling up every fireball the trees threw the Skylanders' way. Soon he was full to bursting. Meanwhile, Grim Creeper was struggling to get near the trees without being beaten back by their burning branches. Even the ghost's black tunic was smoldering from the heat.

Slam Bam wasn't doing much better. His ice defenses were melting faster than he could build them.

"Eruptor!" he shouted. "Can't you fight fire with fire?"

But the lava monster just looked sick. "I ate too much," he said, barfing up a pool of magma that nearly fried Grim Creeper's feet. "Sorry!"

The reaper hardly even noticed. He was too busy trying to avoid the red-hot roots that were breaking out of the ground and rearing up like snakes. The flaming trees were on the move, and there was nowhere to run.

"GET THEM!" the trees shouted as they

closed in on the Skylanders.

Slam Bam made some icy boxing gloves to protect his fists as he tried to smash the advancing plants, while Eruptor had recovered enough to spit some magma balls left, right, and center. But it wasn't helping. The trees simply batted the magma balls right back where they came from. Even Grim Creeper became entangled in the burning roots, unable to reach his scythe, let alone swing it.

It was hopeless. The Skylanders were outnumbered and outflanked.

They were going to meet a fiery end thousands of years before they'd even been born!

Chapter Seven

The Last of the Portal Masters

"This is getting too hot to handle!" yelled Slam Bam as a fiery branch whacked him on the back, singeing his fur.

"Even for me!" admitted Eruptor, who was now wrestling with a flaming tree. There was only one choice left. He could erupt into a giant lake of lava, but then he'd scald his friends as much as the trees—and the burning wood warriors might even enjoy it!

This couldn't be how it ended. Not here, not now, in the dim and distant past. What would happen to Master Eon in the future if they failed? What would happen to Skylands?

The thought of Kaos winning was too much to bear. Eruptor could almost hear the evil Portal Master cackling in his head.

The heat was intense. Flames raged in from every angle. Behind Eruptor, Slam Bam was shouting. In front, Grim Creeper was disappearing underneath a mass of glowing roots.

Then Eruptor realized it wasn't the roots that were glowing—it was the air around the reaper. Eruptor's eyes widened. It was a Portal of Power. Grim Creeper was being transported out of danger.

Eruptor twisted and saw Slam Bam dissolve in another flash of light. One moment the yeti was there, the next he was gone. Where were they going? Was Master Eon dragging them back to the future already?

And what about him?

Eruptor's question was answered with a bump when he landed on the floor of a gloomy cave. Torches burned weakly on the rocky walls, sending shadows flickering around the cavern.

He wasn't alone. Slam Bam and Grim Creeper rushed over to see if he was all right. Eruptor brushed off their concern with a question of his own.

"Where are we?" he asked. "This isn't Master Eon's citadel."

Before his friends could answer, a voice echoed around the cave.

"Who is Master Eon? And who are you?"

Eruptor pushed himself to his feet. "Great! Just what we need—a spooky and mysterious voice!"

"You will answer the question!" the voice insisted.

"Which one?" shrugged Slam Bam.

"Um," said the voice, suddenly not quite as impressive as before. "The first one!"

"Eon is our Portal Master," Grim Creeper offered, raising his scythe just in case the spooky and mysterious voice was attached to an equally spooky and mysterious body.

"Impossible," it shouted back. "The Portal Masters are no more! And who do you claim to be?"

"We claim to be what we are!" said Eruptor. "Skylanders—and proud of it!"

"Now I know you are lying," the voice screamed. "The Skylanders have been banished. They, too, are gone!"

"Well, your Skylanders may have scrammed, but not us!" said Slam Bam. "We're from the future!"

"The future?" said a smaller voice behind them. The Skylanders whirled around to see a tiny hunched figure leaning on a rickety staff. It was a particularly ancient-looking Mabu, wearing a huge pair of glasses.

"Where did you come from?" Eruptor asked, secretly thanking his lucky stars that he hadn't barfed lava all over the Mabu's sandaled feet.

"I was here the whole time," the Mabu

replied, his voice as dry as old leaves. "I just made myself invisible."

"You can do that?" asked Slam Bam.

The Mabu twitched his nose and vanished to prove it. A moment later he reappeared.

"And the voice?" asked Grim Creeper.

"ALSO ME!" boomed the Mabu, magically bouncing his words off the moss-covered rocks.

"Nice!" the reaper admitted.

"Thanks," said the Mabu, trying a weak smile. "I still know a few tricks, even at my age."

"Are you a wizard?" Eruptor asked.

The Mabu drew himself up to his full height, which, to be honest, wasn't very tall. "No, lava monster. My name is Wizbit. I am a Portal Master."

Slam Bam frowned. "But you said . . ."

"I'm the last Portal Master. My brothers and sisters have all fled Skylands. I alone remained to defeat the Nightmare King." Wizbit's furry face crumpled in sorrow. "I failed!"

"Well, don't be hard on yourself, small fry," Eruptor said kindly.

"Yeah," agreed Slam Bam. "We hear he's a pretty bogus dude!"

"Then you heard right," Wizbit said. "He defeated the Skylanders—our Skylanders— and enslaved every race on Skylands. Mabu. Gillmen. Molekin. Kangarats. Even dragons.

None can stand against him. Not even you—even if you wanted to!"

"Of course we want to," insisted Grim Creeper. "That's why we've been sent back here."

"That's what he said you'd say," Wizbit said sadly.

"Who?" asked Eruptor.

"Me!" announced a new voice from the other side of the cave.

Before the Skylanders could turn, Wizbit twitched his nose. "I'm sorry," he said as magical golden ropes appeared around the champions, binding them together.

"Hey, what are you doing?" Slam Bam asked as he struggled against the bonds. Eruptor was also trying to free himself, but he felt so weak all of a sudden. It was almost as if his fire was going out. Grim Creeper's ghostly spirit turned feeble inside his armor.

"He's doing what I asked him to, FOOLS!" said the owner of the voice, stepping out of the shadows.

"Kaos!" Eruptor spat.

"The very same," Kaos gloated, turning his attention to the wrinkled Mabu. "You have done well, my friend."

"Your friend?" Slam Bam couldn't believe what he was hearing. "Wizbit, do you know who this is?"

"Of course he does, FOOL!" interrupted Kaos. "He knows that I, KAOOOOS, have come from the future to help him defeat Nefarion."

Chapter Eight

Big Bad Ice Bomb

Grim Creeper couldn't believe what he was hearing. "Wizbit," the reaper pleaded. "He's tricking you. Surely you can see that?"

The Mabu scratched behind his ear with his staff. "All I know is that Kaos told me that you would arrive, claiming to be Skylanders. Claiming to be my friends."

"We are," said Eruptor.

"Liars!" snapped Kaos. "I know you are agents of the Nightmare King, sent to capture brave Wizbit and stop him from carrying out his plan. I know the truth."

"Truth?" exploded Eruptor. "You wouldn't know the truth if it crept up and bit you on the bottom!"

"You leave my bottom out of this!" Kaos yelled. "Evil burns in your hearts, all three of you. I know it, and so does little Wizbit here."

"Burns in my heart?" Eruptor scoffed, unable to keep his temper under control anymore. He was steaming, quite literally. "I'll show you what burning really means."

A deep rumble could be heard from Eruptor's body. The other two Skylanders tried to inch away from their fiery friend, knowing what was about to happen. Eruptor was about to live up to his name and erupt into a pool of boiling lava. It would be worth it. As soon as the magma burned through Wizbit's rope they would be able to teach Kaos a lesson once and for all.

Eruptor screamed, the rumbling reaching a climax. "I came, I saw—and I burned!"

Slam Bam screwed his eyes shut, ready for

the scalding lava to roll over him, but nothing happened. He opened one eye to check, but could only see Kaos snicker to himself.

"What's the matter, Eruptor?" the evil Portal Master asked. "Get cut off in full flow?"

"I—I don't understand," Eruptor said, looking down at the ropes as they glistened in the gloom of the cave. "Why can't I erupt?"

"Those ropes do more than bind you," Wizbit explained sadly. "They stop you from using your powers."

"You are as helpless as a newborn sugar bat!" Kaos sneered. "Finally, I have you where I want you, FOOLS!"

"See?" said Grim Creeper, pleading with Wizbit to believe them. "Kaos just wants to stop us from stopping him. He's using you, Wizbit. Don't trust him!"

Wizbit looked at his accomplice. "Do they speak the truth, Kaos? Are you just using me?"

Kaos rested a hand on the Mabu's shoulder.

"See how they seek to confuse you, old friend? If I was using you, why would I have promised to sneak you inside King Nefarion's castle?"

"He's promised you *what?*" Slam Bam asked.

Wizbit looked down at his sandals. "I shouldn't say."

"No," Kaos said. "Do it. Talk me through your BRILLIANT plan, one more time."

Wizbit looked nervously at the Skylanders, who were still trying to break out of the impossibly tight ropes. "You mean, in front of them?"

"They are powerless," jeered Kaos. "Thanks to you. Tell them how you will defeat their master once and for all! Tell them how they've FAILED!"

Wizbit nodded. "Very well." He wiggled his nose and a bomb appeared in the air, floating in front of him. Its surface was covered in frost, and icicles hung from its smooth bottom.

"This is the Big Bad Ice Bomb," Wizbit explained. "One of Skylands' most Legendary Treasures. It took me years, but I finally tracked it down."

Slam Bam couldn't help but be intrigued.

Like all yetis, he was fascinated with anything connected to ice. "What does it do?"

Wizbit still didn't look sure about revealing his plan, but with a little coaxing from Kaos he continued. "Once detonated, it will freeze Nefarion and his infernal kingdom in eternal winter. Skylands will be free of his tyranny forever!"

"Once inside the Nightmare King's castle," Kaos said smugly, "Wizbit will sneak the bomb under Nefarion's throne. The Nightmare King is DOOOOOMED!" Kaos smiled at the aged Portal Master. It was the kind of smile that could curdle milk. "Isn't that right, Wizbit, old buddy, old pal?"

The Mabu nodded, but Kaos wasn't finished yet. "No, say it out loud, Master Wizbit. That's what you plan to do, isn't it?"

Eruptor felt his lava itching. Something was wrong here.

"Y-yes," confirmed Wizbit—and the walls started rumbling.

Actually, that's an understatement: The walls started shaking. Violently. Stones tumbled from the high ceiling as deep cracks appeared all around the cavern.

"W-what's happening?" squeaked Wizbit.

"Oh, it's nothing." Kaos smirked. "Just more of my friends arriving."

Behind him, boulders started rolling from the walls and joining together. They were forming into huge, hulking moss-covered figures.

"Wait a minute," said Eruptor. "Those walls aren't even walls!"

"Correct, lava breath," cackled Kaos. "Meet the Stony Stone Golems of DOOM!"

Chapter Nine

The Stony Stone Golems of *Doom* !

The Stony Stone Golems stomped past Kaos and formed a circle around the tiny form of Wizbit. The trembling Mabu squeaked as a massive hand closed around his trembling body, plucking him from the ground.

"Let go of me," he pleaded. "I don't understand what's happening."

"Kaos has double-crossed you," Slam Bam said with a snarl. "That's what!"

"But why?" wailed the furry Portal Master. "You said you were my friend! You said you would help me defeat Nefarion!"

Kaos pretended to be shocked, batting

his evil eyelashes. "Me?" he gasped in mock surprise. "Help you defeat my master?"

Eruptor did a double take. "Your *what*? Since when did Kaos serve anyone?"

"Since I met the Nightmare King," announced Kaos. "Since I met the most evil person who ever existed. A monarch so menacing that he makes my own mother look like a Fluffkin. Behold, your lord and master. Behold, NEFARIOOOOON!"

The air above Kaos shimmered and a gigantic head appeared, glowing the sort of green shade most people only turn when they're feeling queasy. It was bigger than Kaos's own beloved giant head and twice as ugly, if such a thing was possible.

This was probably because the head was wearing the Mask of Power, not broken into eight pieces but complete. It was more hideous than Eruptor had imagined, encircled by a mane of snakes that writhed and hissed, spraying venom from their needle-like fangs.

This was Nefarion, the Nightmare King—and by the look of him, he more than lived up to his name!

"Master," Kaos simpered, dropping to one knee. "How marvelous to look upon your wickedness again."

"SLAVE KAOS," Nefarion thundered. "YOU HAVE SERVED US WELL!" The voice was like a thousand noisy dragons roaring at once.

"Thank you, your Horrendous Majesty," Kaos said, bowing even lower. "Did you hear what the traitor Wizbit said he was going to do to you?"

"WE DID!" replied the Nightmare King. "HE PLOTS TO FREEZE US IN ETERNAL WINTER!" The head broke into maniacal laughter. "HE IS A FOOL!"

"The most foolish of fools," agreed Kaos. "But I, KAOS, have delivered him to you!"

"I am a fool," Wizbit agreed from within the Stone Golem's tight grasp. His voice was stronger than it had sounded before, and Eruptor noticed that his eyes were dancing with defiance. "I am a fool to allow myself to be taken in, and maybe even a fool to believe that I could beat you. But, as long as there is breath in my body, I will keep trying."

"VERY WELL," boomed Nefarion. Dark lightning flashed from his beady eyes, striking Wizbit in the chest. The Mabu cried out before falling silent, his body slumped over in the Golem's fist.

"No!" yelled Eruptor. He strained against his bonds, turning to face Nefarion's head. "You're nothing but a big bully. Why don't you pick on someone your own size?"

"LIKE YOU, LITTLE LAVA ANT?" the Nightmare King mocked. He rocked with terrible laughter once again. "YOU ARE NOTHING COMPARED TO US! NOTHING!"

"We've heard it all before, Big Head," scoffed Slam Bam, fixing Kaos with a hard stare. "And it always ends the same way."

Kaos smirked at the yeti before spinning on his heel. "Don't listen to them, my lord. They are just SKYLOSERS, every last one of them."

Nefarion looked quizzical for a minute. "SKY-WHAT?"

"Um, I said sly losers," Kaos quickly corrected himself. "Insignificant worms—although to be honest, that's being unfair to worms."

"ALL ARE WORMS IN OUR PRESENCE!" the Nightmare King bellowed.

"Oh, you do go on, don't you?" Kaos hissed beneath his breath, his sickening smile never slipping for a second.

"Now you know how we feel," muttered Eruptor.

"GOLEMS, BRING THE PORTAL MASTER TO US!" Nefarion ordered. "HE SHALL BE PUNISHED FOR HIS

TREACHERY." The Nightmare King fixed his eyes upon Kaos. "AND AS FOR YOU . . ."

"Yes?" Kaos asked, distinctly less confident than he had been before.

"BRING US THIS ICE BOMB. WE WISH TO EXAMINE IT!"

Relieved, Kaos bowed. "As you command, Your Repugnant Majesty!"

"ALL SHALL SERVE THE NIGHTMARE KING!" the head boomed before vanishing, taking Wizbit and the Stony Stone with him.

"Weeeeeeell," said Kaos, rubbing his hands together in glee. "What shall we do now, FOOOOOLS?"

Eruptor gritted his teeth. "How about I burn through these rocks and then smother you in lava?" the lava monster suggested.

"Oh yes, the ropes. How's that working out for you?" Kaos said with a sneer.

Eruptor looked down to see that his lava

was having little effect on the golden cords. Beside him, Slam Bam was growling with frustration as his ice just slipped off the ropes. Only Grim Creeper remained quiet. The reaper had managed to snatch a sharp stone from the cave floor and was busy sawing it back and forth across the cords behind his back.

"Those ropes are resistant to magic tricks as well as extreme temperatures, SKYBLUNDERERS," Kaos cackled. "Not even a Fire Viper could burn its way free."

"What are you going to do with us?" asked Grim Creeper, getting straight to the point.

"Do?" retorted Kaos innocently, an evil smirk creeping across his horrible face. "Me? Why, absolutely nothing! Why would I want to do anything to three of my worst enemies, especially when A) they are tied up in a deep, dark cavern, miles underground; B) they are trapped five thousand years in the past, and; C) they're about to be crushed beneath a freak cave-in?"

"What cave-in?" asked Eruptor, his superheated heart sinking.

"*This* cave-in," Kaos replied, firing a bolt of energy from his fingers. It hit the cave roof, loosening the already unstable walls.

Rocks began to rain down as Kaos snapped his fingers and Portalled away with the Ice Bomb. "Bye-bye, SKYLOSERS. We won't meet again. Mostly because you will be BURIED ALIVE! Bwa-ha-ha-HAAAAAAA!"

Kaos's rotten laughter was drowned out by the roar of the roof collapsing on the three helpless heroes.

Chapter Ten

Buried Alive

"Okay, that could have gone better," admitted Slam Bam as the rocks settled above them.

"No kidding!" replied Eruptor.

"Well, at least we haven't been crushed," pointed out Grim Creeper, trying to keep the mood light (which can be difficult when you're buried beneath several thousand tons of heavy rock).

The reaper had a point though. At the last moment, as the roof had tumbled down, Grim Creeper had managed to saw through Wizbit's magic rope. The golden cord had fallen away, restoring the Skylanders' powers and giving Slam Bam just enough time to throw up an ice shield. Talk about a narrow escape!

The problem was the yeti had no idea how long the instant igloo could hold up the weight of the cave-in. It was holding for now, but was already starting to creak ominously thanks to the incredible weight bearing down on it. Plus, it was starting to melt thanks to Eruptor's natural heat.

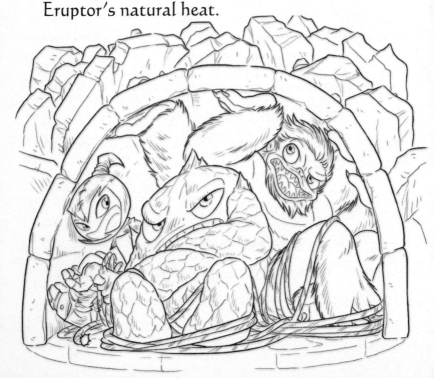

It wouldn't last long.

Slam Bam tapped against one of the slippery ice blocks. "I guess I could create some icy supports for the ceiling," he suggested.

"Where?" asked Eruptor. "There isn't enough room to swing a chili dog in here."

It was true. The Skylanders could hardly move without elbowing one another in the face.

"So, what's the plan?" asked Grim Creeper.

"Simple," said Eruptor. "We escape this inescapable prison, follow Kaos to the Nightmare King's palace, and stop him from taking the mask."

Grim Creeper broke into a smile. "Excellent. And how do we escape?"

Eruptor shrugged. "Yeah, I'm still working that bit out."

"We could tunnel our way out," Grim Creeper suggested.

"If we don't get crushed first," said Slam

Bam, scratching his head.

"Eruptor could burn through the rocks," Grim prompted.

"Yeah, but only after I burned through you two in the process," sighed Eruptor. "Look, kid. You did well, cutting through that rope, but until we can think of an escape plan that doesn't involve us being pulverized between rocks—"

"Or you grilling us by mistake," added Slam Bam.

"—we have to accept that we're stuck here."

"Are you giving up?" Grim said, not quite believing what he was hearing.

"Of course not!" Eruptor said. "We're just temporarily out of ideas, but we'll get there. We're Skylanders, and Skylanders never give up. Not even when we're buried alive."

Grim Creeper's face lit up. "That's it! Eruptor, you're a genius!"

"I am?" Eruptor asked, sounding as if

he didn't quite believe it. "I mean, of course I am." He leaned closer to Grim Creeper, which was quite an achievement as they were pretty close in the first place. "Why, exactly?"

"You said we were buried alive," Grim said, repeating Eruptor's words. "But we're not—not all of us, anyway."

"Did you get hit by a rock when the ceiling caved in, buddy?" asked Slam Bam, looking concerned.

The spooky Skylander laughed. "No! You two are buried alive, but I'm buried Undead! I'm a ghost, remember? And I can do this!"

As his friends watched in amazement, Grim Creeper slipped out of his leather armor and floated in front of them in all of his ghostly glory. "When I'm in my armor, I'm as solid as you two . . . ," he said.

"Or these rocks!" realized Eruptor.

The ghost nodded. "But, when I'm like this, I can slip through the cave-in as easily as a hot scythe through Rotting Robbies."

Slam Bam punched the air, accidentally punching Eruptor at the same time, but the lava monster didn't mind. "Good thinking, kid!"

"I'll get up to the surface and find help!"

"From who?" asked Eruptor.

"I'll head to Nefarion's castle," the ghost replied. "There must be someone there who doesn't like the Nightmare King. You two stay here. I'll be back in no time."

With that, Grim Creeper's ghost was gone, slipping easily through Slam Bam's igloo and disappearing into the rock.

"'Stay here'?" Eruptor repeated. "Where does he think we'll go?"

Beside them Grim Creeper's empty armor shrugged, the hood and gloves floating in the air as if the Undead Skylander was still inside.

"Okay," Slam Bam said with a shiver. "That's just spooky."

Chapter Eleven

The Wailing Walls

"Wahoo!" Grim Creeper's ghost shouted as he appeared above the ground. "I'm a free spirit!"

He had found himself in a storm-lashed valley. A rain forest lay behind him, but his target was ahead.

A massive castle rose into the stormy sky. Its jutting towers were illuminated by lightning between the heavy clouds. Grim Creeper set off, floating over the barren wasteland that surrounded the castle. The Undead Skylander hailed from the Underworld, one of the most terrifying places in all of Skylands, but even he was unnerved by this place. He could almost taste the evil in the air—and all because Nefarion had the Mask of Power. Grim Creeper didn't want to imagine what terror Kaos could unleash if he managed to wrestle the mask from the Nightmare King.

It wasn't just the atmosphere that was making Grim Creeper nervous. As he approached the formidable fortress he realized he could hear mournful voices singing the saddest of songs. It was only when he neared the black battlements that he realized where the singing was coming from.

The bricks that made up the massive walls were carved into the shapes of singing skulls. Grim Creeper couldn't tell if their dreadful song was just to frighten away attackers, or whether the bricks really were that sad. Either way, it didn't do much to raise his spirits. For a moment, he even considered turning around and floating away as fast as he could.

Grim Creeper frowned. *Don't be such a silly spook,* he scolded himself. *You've been in scarier places than this. The other guys are depending on you. You can't let them down.*

Closing his eyes, the Undead Skylander sped up and passed through the Wailing Wall.

Inside, the Nightmare King's castle was even colder than the chilly air outside. Grim slipped down a corridor, passing portraits of Nefarion's ancestors. Have you ever felt like the eyes of a painting are following you around a room? In this case, they did exactly that. The portraits' eyes tumbled out of their painted heads and bounced after the reaper.

"That's just weird," said Grim Creeper, escaping through the soft, thick carpet on the floor.

He appeared in a corridor below, and breathed a sigh of relief that there wasn't a portrait in sight. That said, the décor wasn't much better. The walls were lined with skeletons hanging from chains. Each skeleton was sobbing uncontrollably.

"What's wrong with you?" Grim Creeper asked the nearest bonehead.

"What's wrong with me?" The skeleton wept. "I've been hanging here for five hundred years, and I've got itchy ribs. Do you know what it's like not being able to scratch for five centuries?"

Grim Creeper looked at the skeleton sadly. "I'm sorry," he said. "There's not much I can do without my armor."

"That's okay." The skeleton sniffed. "There is one thing you can do for us, though."

"Anything!" Grim Creeper said, always eager to help.

"Feed our bats!" the skeleton screamed, opening its mouth wide. A swarm of squeaking bats shot out of the skeleton's open jaws, flapping around Grim Creeper's phantom face.

Soon, the air was full of the vicious

creatures, which snapped at the reaper with razor-sharp teeth.

"Ow!" he yelled as one nipped his cheek. Unbelievable! They could bite him even when he was in his ghost form. This place really was a nightmare.

On the walls, the skeletons rattled with laughter.

"Talk about tickling your funny bone!" the one with the itch said with a snort.

Its toothless neighbor agreed. "I'm laughing my skull off here!" it said, snickering.

Grim Creeper didn't find it funny. The bats stayed with him, continuing to bite him, no matter how fast he twisted and turned. Then the ghost had an idea. "Let's see if you really will follow me everywhere, my flappy little friends."

The Skylander did a loop-the-loop in the air and rushed down the corridor, the bats following in hot pursuit. He lurched toward the wall, sweeping through the skeletons. He grinned as the bats did the same, smashing the cackling bone bags into pieces.

The toothless skeleton's skull bounced off the floor one time, before coming to rest next to the rib cage of its itchy neighbor.

"Ooh, yeah," said the first skeleton. "Scratch there! Scratch there!"

Grim Creeper, meanwhile, had reached the end of the corridor, the bats still snapping at his tail. With a last burst of speed, he passed through the wall and finally came to a halt as he heard the bats hitting the bricks on the other side.

Thud. Thud. Thud. Thud.

"Ha!" Grim Creeper laughed. "Maybe next time you'll think twice before trying to snack on a spirit!"

Thankfully, this new corridor was free of paintings and skeletons. It stretched into the distance, its peeling wallpaper interrupted only by the occasional door or arch. There was something else, too. A horribly familiar voice drifted toward the ghost.

"Kaos!" Grim Creeper muttered beneath his breath and floated toward the sound of the Skylanders' archenemy.

He found the evil Portal Master behind one of the wooden doors. Glumshanks was there, too, holding the Big Bad Ice Bomb in his shaking hands. Unseen, Grim Creeper silently drifted through the door and hid behind a big wooden chest to listen.

"Careful, Glumshanks," hissed Kaos. "You don't want it to go off."

"I don't, Lord Kaos," agreed the Troll. "Th-that's the very last thing I want!"

"Now, let me see," said Kaos, pulling a notebook from his sleeve. "Ah yes, here it is. Kaos's Brilliant Plan for Defeating the Nightmare King. Step one: Go back in time."

"Ch-check," said Glumshanks, still nervously clutching the bomb.

"Step two: Obtain the Big Bad Ice Bomb."

"D-d-done."

"Step three: Cast a timing spell that will prime the Big Bad Ice Bomb to detonate in half an hour. Simple enough." Kaos flexed his fingers before focusing on the Legendary Treasure. "Big Bad Ice Bomb! I, KAOS, command you to explode in thirty minutes. Not a second more, not a second less. You will freeze King Nefarion where he stands so I can grab the Mask of Power and become ALL-POWERFUL!"

Kaos stared at the bomb, but nothing happened. Suddenly he remembered the last word of the spell. "Please!"

An eerie blue glow pulsed across the bomb's icy surface, and the spell was cast.

"There," said Kaos, looking immensely pleased with himself. "Now to pass the bomb to the Nightmare King and— BOOOOOM—victory is mine."

"Congratulations, Lord Kaos," Glumshanks said, still not completely convinced that the Legendary Treasure wasn't about to go off in his face.

"If only those Skyblunderers were around to see me triumph," Kaos said, grinning the evil grin he saved for special occasions. "But I think it's best they stay trapped beneath the ground for all time."

You wish, thought Grim Creeper in his hiding place. Unfortunately, there was nothing he could do to wipe that stupid smile from Kaos's smug face. Not while he was still in his ghost form. Unless . . .

Now it was Grim Creeper's turn to grin. A plan had formed in his spectral head, but he had to move quickly. He had only half an hour before the Big Bad Ice Bomb went *boom!*

Chapter Twelve

Cell Break

At the bottom of the Nightmare King's nightmarish fortress lay the dungeons.

The dungeons, like the rest of the castle, were not a nice place to hang out. They were made worse by the fact that they were just above the sewers (which held the title of Skylands' Smelliest Location until Kaos's sock drawer was invented nearly five thousand years later).

It was in these dungeons that the last of the Portal Masters sat, feeling extremely sorry for himself. Wizbit slumped on a bumpy, worn-out mattress, staring at his feet with such fury that you would think it was his toes' fault he had fallen for Kaos's lies.

"How could I have been so stupid?" the old Mabu said out loud.

"Don't blame yourself," replied a spooky voice.

"AAAAAAAAARGH!" screamed the nervy Portal Master.

"Sorry about that!" said Grim Creeper, slipping effortlessly through the dungeon wall. "Scaring folk goes with the territory when you're a ghost. Even a friendly one!"

"I deserve to be scared," the Mabu said sadly. "I was such a fool. I can't believe I blew my chance to stop Nefarion!"

"There's still a way," said Grim Creeper, floating excitedly in front of the Portal Master.

"There is?" asked Wizbit.

Grim Creeper explained how Eruptor and Slam Bam were trapped with his living armor beneath the ground.

"If you Portalled them out," the reaper concluded, "we could send Kaos back to the future and help you defeat Nefarion."

"You'd do that for me?" said the Mabu. "Even after I betrayed you?"

"Of course we would," Grim Creeper said. "You're a Portal Master. We're Skylanders. Helping you is what we do."

"There's only one small problem," pointed out Wizbit. "I can't do anything without a Portal of Power. There's one in Nefarion's throne room, but that's upstairs, and we're all the way down here. How are we even going to get out of this dungeon?"

A smile lit up Grim Creeper's face. "I was hoping you were going to ask me that!"

Outside the Portal Master's cell, a large, heavily armored Troll was eating his lunch. It was his favorite—a pebble and seaweed sandwich. Lip-smackingly delicious.

He was about to take a bite when his

prisoner shouted through the gap at the bottom of the cell door.

"Hello out there," Wizbit cried.

"What do you want?" the Troll replied with a snarl, the sandwich almost at his thick, blubbery lips. "I'm on my break!"

"I was just wondering if you could clear something up for me?" asked the Portal Master.

"No!" the Troll snapped and took a big bite, crunching the pebbles noisily. *Mmm. Delicious.*

"It's just that I've heard these dungeons are haunted," Wizbit continued anyway. "Is that true?"

The Troll stopped chewing. "Haunted?"

"Yes," replied the Portal Master. "By a ghost who really, really doesn't like Trolls."

The Troll swallowed nervously. "Sounds pretty ridiculous to me."

"You're probably right," agreed Wizbit. "Besides, they say the phantom only attacks when a Troll is eating. Thanks for the chat!"

The prisoner fell quiet, and the Troll looked suspiciously at his half-eaten sandwich. *Nah!* The old Mabu didn't know what he was talking about. It was just an old story.

Wasn't it?

Something whistled past the Troll's lumpy head.

The guard jumped to his feet, dropping his sandwich. The pebbles rolled away—only to be blown back seconds later.

"Aaargh!" screamed the Troll, snatching up what he hoped was his sword but turned out to be the keys to the cell. He brandished them in front of himself, shouting into the shadows. "Who's there?"

Another breeze whooshed across his back. He whirled around, just in time to spot something passing through the wall into the cells.

"Who's there?" he shrieked.

"Sorry?" Wizbit responded innocently.

"No one here but me. Oh, and the ghost."

"The ghost?" the Troll asked, his voice wavering as his eyes darted around the dungeon. "You mean it's real?"

In answer to his question, voices came from every direction at once.

"Troll. Troll. Troll."

"Leave me alone!" yelled the guard.

"TROLL. TROLL. TROLL."

"I don't believe in you!" the Troll cried. "You don't exist!"

Suddenly the voices stopped and the dungeon was still. No wind. No noise. Nothing.

"Oh, so you don't believe in the ghost, huh?" Wizbit asked.

"No," insisted the Troll, now attempting to hide behind the keys. "No, I do not."

"That's too bad," said the Mabu. "Because he believes in you!"

A spectral face appeared in front of the Troll, its eyes flashing in the dark.

"Boo!" the ghost said with a grin.

"Waaaaaaaaaah!" the Troll wailed, throwing down the keys and running for his life. "I want my mommy!"

The rest of Grim Creeper's body appeared beneath his head, and he watched as the guard vanished out the main dungeon gate. Then he floated down to the discarded ring of keys and blew it beneath Wizbit's cell door.

Seconds later, the Portal Master had unlocked the door and was free. Of course, there was still the issue of how they were going to sneak into the throne room.

"Not a problem," said the ghostly Skylander, pointing at a spare suit of armor lying in a pile against the dungeon wall. "Have you ever wanted to be a Troll?"

Chapter Thirteen

The Throne Room of Terror

"This will never work," puffed Wizbit, clanking down a corridor in the ridiculously large armor.

"Yes, it will," encouraged Grim Creeper, floating ahead. "Just think like a Troll."

Unable to see out from beneath the heavy helmet, Wizbit walked into a stone pillar with a *crash*.

"That's more like it!" said the ghost.

They turned a corner and found themselves in the far end of the throne room. It was a huge chamber, full of diamond statues and creepy tapestries. Grim Creeper hadn't even realized that tapestries could be so creepy until he saw this nightmarish needlework. Each tapestry showed King Nefarion stamping on a creature. Mabu, Molekin, even cyclopses—they were all getting squashed beneath the Nightmare King's boots.

And there, sitting on a gigantic throne made out of bones, was Nefarion himself. He looked like a spider lurking at the center of its web, long arms and legs sprouting from a thin, wiry body that was almost as bony as the throne itself. On his face he wore the Mask of Power, which was just as horrific as it had been in Wizbit's cavern. The mane of serpents writhed around Nefarion's head, tiny tongues tasting the air.

"Look," said Wizbit, struggling to point in the hefty armor. "It's Kaos."

Sure enough, the evil Portal Master was approaching the throne. Glumshanks, holding the Big Bad Ice Bomb, followed behind.

"We're too late," whispered the Mabu.

But Grim Creeper had spotted something else on the other side of the room. "It's the Portal of Power," he said, trying to work out how they could reach it without being seen.

"Your Frightful Majesty," Kaos began, bowing in front of the Nightmare King. "I bring you the Big Bad Ice Bomb, as commanded."

"We thank you, loyal and worthless servant," hissed Nefarion, indicating for Glumshanks to come forward. The Troll

looked nervously at his master and
then shuffled toward the throne.

"That's close enough," the king ordered,
raising a hand. Glumshanks came to a halt,
nearly falling over his large feet.

"Interesting," the king wheezed, cocking
his head to listen to the Legendary Treasure.
"Can you hear anything, Kaos?"

Kaos thrust out his bottom lip. "Nothing
at all, Your Monstrous Majesty. Can you,
Glumshanks?"

The Troll shook his head. "No, Lord Kaos."

"We can," the king announced, anger flooding into his voice. "The Big Bad Ice Bomb. It's ticking!"

"No!" exclaimed Kaos, his mouth dropping open in mock surprise. "Why would it be doing that?"

"Treachery!" cried Nefarion. "Do you think we are a fool?"

"Wellllll . . ." Kaos smirked. "Now that I come to think of it . . ."

"You have cast a timing spell on this weapon," said the king. "We can smell it. You plan to freeze us in our own castle, just like that pathetic Portal Master."

"And it's a plan that will work!" Kaos screamed, throwing his hands above his head. The Big Bad Ice Bomb shot from Glumshanks' grasp and flew into the air, stopping high above the Nightmare King's throne. "Unless you hand the Mask of Power over to me,

KAOS, you are *DOOOOOMED!*"

"Never," said the king, rising to his feet. Dark energy was already crackling around his claw-like hands, ready to strike down the double-crossing Portal Master where he stood. "We shall destroy you!"

"He's done for!" Wizbit said, but Grim Creeper wasn't too sure.

"Kaos has usually got a trick or two up his sleeves," the ghost said. "Unfortunately."

The Skylander was right. "Destroy me?" Kaos jeered. "You wouldn't know where to start!"

The evil Portal Master clapped his hands together, and in a flash the entire throne room was filled with perfect copies of Kaos, dancing around in victory.

"There are hundreds of them!" Wizbit gasped.

"But which is the real one?" Grim Creeper asked.

It was a question that was obviously

vexing the Nightmare King as well. Nefarion threw balls of energy into the crowd, vaporizing a dozen Kaoses at a time. Every time, more Kaos clones appeared in their place.

"Missed me!" cried a Kaos from the king's right.

"Or did you?" shouted a Kaos to the left.

"By the time you've found the real me," crowed a Kaos from behind the throne, "you'll be as cold as ice."

"Unless you give me that mask!" added another Kaos at the back of the room.

"Your choice," every Kaos said at once, "Your FOOLISH Majesty!"

"Noooooo!" the Nightmare King roared in frustration. The Big Bad Ice Bomb carried on ticking, high above his head.

Chapter Fourteen

Total Kaos

The Nightmare King's throne room was in, well, chaos. Nefarion was ranting and raving, blasting Kaos clones everywhere you looked. The Kaoses, meanwhile, were cackling and crowing and telling anyone who would listen that the Nightmare King was DOOOOMED!

It was just the confusion Grim Creeper and Wizbit needed. Discarding the Mabu's Troll armor, they made their way through the crowd of Kaoses, heading for the Portal of Power. It was the most dangerous thing Wizbit had ever done, and he squealed with

fear every time one of the king's energy balls exploded nearby.

"Don't worry," Grim said, encouraging the little Mabu. "We're nearly there!"

At one point Wizbit was thrown from his feet by a bolt of black lightning that disintegrated the nearest gaggle of laughing Kaoses. Before the Mabu had time to scrabble to his little feet, new Kaoses appeared, taunting the Nightmare King with cries of "Ooh, that tickles!"

"That's it!" shouted Grim Creeper as they reached the Portal. "Now, bring them back! Bring them back now!"

In the cave, the situation had gone from bad to something even worse than worse.

The weight of the cave-in was proving too much for Slam Bam's ice defenses. No sooner did he throw up more ice blocks than they shattered.

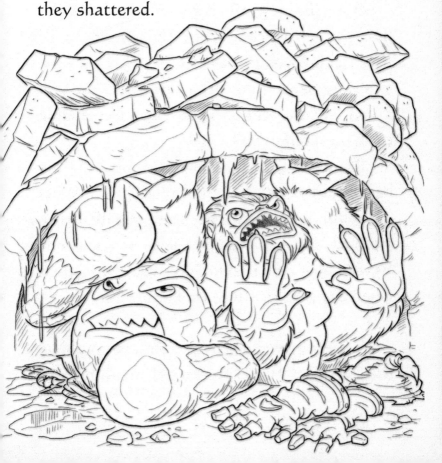

The Skylanders were being squashed into the ground. Eruptor was carefully trying to burn a tunnel through the rock without burning Slam Bam, but without his full lava power, he could only make small gaps at a time.

"It's no good," he said, barely able to move. "I can't get through."

Slam Bam strained to twist toward the living armor, which was now flattened beneath a particularly large rock.

"Any news from Grim Creeper?" the yeti asked, but the leather hood wasn't even able to shake itself in reply.

"Bummer!" Slam Bam said, pushing his back against the rocks. Maybe, just maybe, he could hold back the stones with brute strength alone. It was hopeless, he knew, but Skylanders never, ever gave up. Not even when the situation was this grim.

Wizbit waved his stubby little arms above the Portal of Power. It blazed into life, and three figures appeared out of nowhere.

"Whoa!" cried out Slam Bam as he tumbled back, suddenly freed from the weight of several thousand tons of rock.

"Grim! You did it!" Eruptor cheered, leaping to his feet as the ghost beamed proudly.

"Wizbit did it," Grim Creeper replied, racing back into his living armor and sweeping up his scythe. "That's better. I feel half-alive now!"

Wizbit glanced apologetically at the lava monster. "I am sorry," he said. "I should have listened to you about Kaos."

"Don't sweat it," the Fire Skylander responded, although his eyes widened when he saw the army of Kaoses advancing on the Nightmare King's throne. "And I thought one of him was bad enough!"

"We need to find the real deal!" yelled Grim Creeper, leaping into action, his scythe already chopping through the nearest Kaos.

"And stop him getting the Mask!"

"He's gonna get slammed," cheered his yeti friend, all four fists flying as he piled into the crowd of clones.

The Skylanders surged forward, punching, slicing, and lobbing lava balls—not that it did much good. No sooner did a fake Kaos fall than three despicable duplicates would pop up to taunt the heroes.

"The trail's going cold!" Slam Bam said, trapping six Kaoses in icy prisons. "Where is he?"

Eruptor glanced over to the Nightmare King's throne. Multiple Kaoses were creeping up to try to grab the Mask of Power—but only one of them had Glumshanks by his side!

"There he is," roared Eruptor.

"I see him," Grim Creeper shouted. "Let's bring him some grave tidings!"

"I'll clear a path," Eruptor rumbled. "I've been wanting to do this all day! You can't beat the heat!"

Slam Bam and Grim Creeper leaped back onto the Portal of Power as Eruptor blossomed into a huge pool of rolling lava that spread across the throne room in waves.

"Surf's up!" shouted Slam Bam as the magma reached the throne. Creating an iceboard beneath his feet, the yeti launched himself from the Portal and surfed the lava flow, with Grim Creeper hanging on to his white mane.

"What is this?" Nefarion gasped as Slam Bam streaked past.

"Skylanders in action!" yelled Grim Creeper.

"Giving evil the cold shoulder," Slam Bam grinned, piling into the real Kaos and Glumshanks.

But they weren't as real as he thought. The nasty Portal Master disappeared as soon as he was barged, and so did Glumshanks.

"What the—?" shouted Eruptor as he re-formed, but he was interrupted by a gleeful cry of triumph from a Kaos.

The original Kaos.

The victorious Kaos.

"No!" screamed Nefarion as the Mask was yanked from his face. Immediately, he started to shrink. Those extraordinarily long limbs started to shorten. His unsettling body became squat and childlike.

"Not fair!" Nefarion wailed, tears flowing down his now-chubby cheeks.

"Behold!" cried Kaos as his duplicates vanished, their job done. "The Nightmare King revealed!"

"But he's just a boy," gasped Wizbit from the Portal.

"More like a spoiled brat! Why do you think he had the Mask of Power created in the first place? The pampered prince was never taken seriously, even when he was crowned!" Kaos stuck out his bottom lip as he loomed over the kid king. "What's the matter? Has the bad man got your mask?"

Nefarion responded by flying into an almighty temper tantrum.

"So much for the most terrifying tyrant ever to rule Skylands," Slam Bam said.

But Eruptor's eyes were on their greatest enemy. "Kaos!" he yelled. "Drop the mask!"

"I don't think so, SKYLOSER!" Kaos sneered. "I've waited a long time for this."

As the Skylanders watched in horror, Kaos held the mask in the air and began to lower it over his wicked, grinning face.

Chapter Fifteen

The Mask of Power

"I don't think so," roared Eruptor, spitting a magma ball right at Kaos. It hit the mask, and the enchanted wood caught fire immediately.

"HOT!" screeched Kaos, tossing the mask into the air before tumbling off the throne.

Everyone in the throne room watched the blazing mask arc above their heads. Suddenly the sobbing Nightmare King leaped from his seat. "Mine!" he yelled, running to catch the Mask as it started to tumble back to the ground. "I mean, ours!"

"No! It belongs to KAOS!" screamed Kaos, jumping up from where he had fallen.

Even Glumshanks, who had been trying to stay out of the way, raced forward, arms outstretched. "I'll get it for you, my lord!"

The three villains charged together, all eyes on the Mask.

CRUNCH!

Eruptor winced as they plowed straight into one another and landed in a heap on the floor.

Kaos was the first to recover. "Where is it?" he babbled, scrabbling out of the mess of arms and legs. "Where is the mask?"

"It must be here somewhere," said Nefarion, gazing around the floor.

"Ow!" said Glumshanks.

"Are you looking for this?" said a voice from above.

Kaos, Nefarion, and Glumshanks looked up to see Wizbit standing on the shoulders of Grim Creeper, who himself was being held aloft by two of Slam Bam's muscular arms. The Mabu was brandishing the extinguished but charred Mask of Power.

"Give us back our mask," Nefarion ordered, tottering forward only to be stopped by a sudden splash of boiling lava.

"Sorry," grinned Eruptor mischievously. "Indigestion!"

Perched on top of the other Skylanders, Wizbit held the mask as high as he could. "This accursed mask has brought nothing but evil to Skylands. Its reign of terror ends today."

"No!" shouted Kaos. "You mustn't!"

"I must. With the last of my magic I shatter the mask forever," Wizbit replied. "Mask of Power—no more!"

The mask shone as bright as a thousand suns and shattered in front of their eyes. The force of Wizbit's spell sent the Skylanders staggering back, and Slam Bam dropped Grim Creeper to the floor. The Undead Skylander twisted as he fell, and grabbed the Mabu before he hit the stone tiles.

When the glare cleared, the Mask was gone.

"Where is it?" Nefarion bawled. "WHERE IS OUR MASK?"

"Gone!" Eruptor cheered. "Split into eight segments."

"One for each Element," said Slam Bam. "And scattered across Skylands," Grim Creeper added. "Where they will remain hidden."

"For now!" spat Kaos. The Skylanders spun around to face the evil Portal Master. "You forget, SKYBLUNDERERS, I have five of the segments safely tucked away five thousand years in the future."

"Give it up, Kaos!" Eruptor said, advancing on the villain. "You've lost!"

"Kaos never loses!" the Portal Master screeched. "Not when there's a Big Bad Ice Bomb ready to blow! Enjoy being frozen for all time, lava breath. Come, Glumshanks. We're leaving! Back to the future! Back to my VICTORY!"

Kaos clapped his hands together and a time rift appeared behind him, gobbling up the evil Portal Master and Glumshanks before the Skylanders could react.

"The bomb!" wailed Nefarion, going

white with terror. "It's going to go off. Run for your lives!"

The not-so-nightmarish king turned on his heels and fled as fast as his little legs would carry him.

"I'd forgotten about that thing," admitted Slam Bam, looking up at the ticking Legendary Treasure.

"I hadn't," said Grim Creeper, "but it's okay. Wizbit can just diffuse it, right?"

"Wrong," said the Mabu, looking pitiful. "I used the last of my magic to destroy the mask."

"But it's going to go off any minute now!" said Grim Creeper.

Eruptor stepped forward. "It's fine. I know what to do!"

Beside him, Slam Bam realized what the lava monster had in mind. "Eruptor, you can't!"

"Don't you get it, Slam?" Eruptor smiled sadly. "I already have. Give me a hand, okay?"

"I don't understand," Wizbit said, but Grim Creeper just placed a gauntleted hand on the Mabu's shoulder.

"It's all a matter of timing," the ghost said softly as Slam Bam hurled Eruptor into the air.

The lava monster opened his mouth and swallowed the Legendary Treasure in one gulp.

"It could use a little salt," Eruptor said before the Big Bad Ice Bomb exploded in his stomach. The lava monster was instantly encased in a sheet of ice that started to creep slowly toward them.

"I think Nefarion had a point," Slam Bam said, dragging his eyes away from his frozen friend. "RUN!"

The Skylanders ran for their lives.

Chapter Sixteen

A Final Message

In the future, Master Eon took a deep breath. The dizziness had finally passed. That could only mean one thing. Supporting himself with his staff, he closed his eyes and let his mind reach out across Skylands.

There was no Darkness. No Emperor Kaos. Skylands was just as it should be.

"They did it." The Portal Master breathed, opening his eyes again. Of course they had. They never let him down.

Now all he had to do was bring them safely home.

Muttering magical words beneath his

breath, Master Eon slammed the end of his staff onto the ground. In front of him, the rip in time reappeared. He peered into the wild, shimmering colors, calling the Skylanders by name.

Seconds later they tumbled into the Portal room—Slam Bam, Grim Creeper, and an ancient-looking Mabu who looked suspiciously like an older version of his assistant, Hugo.

As soon as they were through, the rift closed forever.

Slam Bam looked up at his Portal Master. "Am I glad to see you!"

"Welcome back, Slam Bam," said Master Eon proudly. "And congratulations. Skylands is safe once more. The true course of history has been restored!"

"But Eruptor," said Grim Creeper. "He's still—"

"Frozen," Master Eon said, his face looking grim. "I know."

"I think I can help with that," Wizbit

chimed in, pushing his frosty glasses up his nose. "My magic may have gone, but I still remember a spell or two. All we need is a Portal Master to say the ancient mystical words."

The Mabu grinned knowingly at Master Eon.

"Master Eon?" said Professor Splinters as the Portal Master appeared with the Skylanders and Wizbit in the middle of the cavern.

"Good to see you back to normal, Professor," said Master Eon as Slam Bam and Grim Creeper rushed forward to check on Eruptor. He was frozen in the exact place they had last seen him, five thousand years earlier.

"Normal?" asked the Treeman. "Why wouldn't I be?"

Master Eon chuckled, turning to the elderly Mabu who had appeared by his side. "You have it?"

Wizbit handed Master Eon the Book of Power. "I wrote it on the back page," the Mabu said. "Words that haven't been spoken in Skylands for millennia."

"Then let's get a move on," said Slam Bam impatiently, before apologizing to Master Eon. The Portal Master merely flipped open the book and began reciting the spell.

"Is it working?" asked Grim Creeper, never taking his eyes off Eruptor.

Slam Bam raised all four hands, and pressed them against the ice. "Yes!" he announced. "The ice is retreating, flowing back into Eruptor's body!"

As they watched, the ice block melted away to nothing, leaving Eruptor hanging in the air. He still looked frozen, his lava an icy blue rather than its usual roaring red, but in the blink of an eye the color returned to his rocky skin. Eruptor crashed back down to the ground and opened his eyes.

"Hey, buddy," Slam Bam said, welcoming

his friend with a sharp-toothed smile. "How are you feeling?"

Eruptor replied by burping out the remains of the Big Bad Ice Bomb.

"Does that answer your question?" Grim Creeper asked.

Behind them, the pages of the Book of Power started to glow. Eruptor frowned at Master Eon. "Hey, doesn't that only happen when it's near a fragment of the mask?"

"Maybe it is," said Master Eon, stretching out a hand. The bomb (or what was left of it) rose magically into the air and transformed into the Fire segment of the Mask of Power.

"Ha!" laughed Wizbit. "Of course. It would have spirited away to the coldest place possible when I broke up the mask!"

"The middle of the Big Bad Ice Bomb!" realized Grim Creeper.

"Which ended up in the middle of him!" Slam Bam laughed and pointed a hairy thumb at Eruptor.

But the lava monster was watching Master Eon. The tall Portal Master wasn't celebrating, but staring at the pages of the Book of Power in despair.

"What's wrong, Master Eon?" the lava monster asked. "We stopped Kaos, right?"

Eon turned the pages so the Skylanders could see. The book was showing an image of Kaos holding the completed mask.

"Ah, stay cool," said Slam Bam. "That's just what happened back in Nefarion's castle. Kaos found the mask too hot to handle."

"No," said Wizbit, peering at the pages. "That's not the past."

"I'm afraid not," Master Eon agreed. "The book is showing us the future."

"What?" asked Eruptor. "You mean . . ."

"I mean," said Master Eon, "that whatever we do, Kaos is destined to wear the Mask of Power. He's going to win!"

To be concluded in . . .

TRIGGER HAPPY

TARGETS THE EVIL KAOS

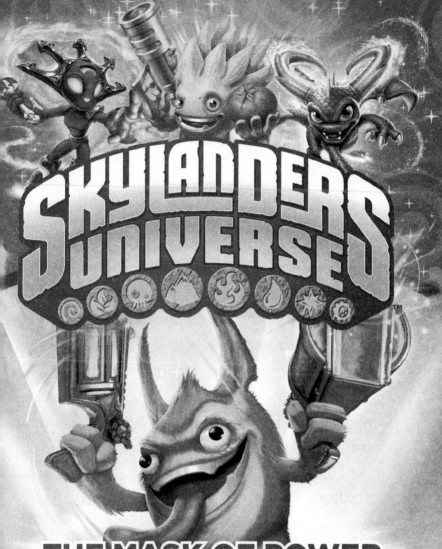

THE MASK OF POWER

TRIGGER HAPPY

TARGETS THE
EVIL KAOS

Chapter One

Snake Attack!

S ince you're reading this book, chances are you've never had to fight a Water Viper. For this, you should count yourself very, very lucky.

Some of you may not even know what a Water Viper is. If that's the case, imagine a snake. One with a wriggly, muscular body and a lot of scales. Oh, and long needle-like fangs, too.

The snake in your head is probably pretty scary, right? The stuff of real nightmares.

Well, a Water Viper is worse. Much worse.

First, take the snake you just imagined

and make it the size of a house. Not a small house—a really big house.

Now, color its scales aqua-blue, and make them super-slimy. Finally, give your snake glowing red eyes and fangs the size of your arm. Actually, make them twice the size of your arm.

If you've done all, that then you're halfway to imagining just how insanely terrifying a Water Viper actually is. Fortunately for you, they don't exist in your world. They live in Skylands, the most magical place in all of creation. Here in Skylands, millions of trillions of gazillions of enchanted islands float in a brilliant blue sky. These islands are filled with amazing creatures and petrifying monsters. Water Vipers fall into the latter category.

Luckily for the people of Skylands, there is a band of heroes who fight monsters and other followers of the Darkness. These are the Skylanders: courageous champions who will stop at nothing to keep Skylands safe from evil.

Courageous champions such as the three who heard a cry for help coming from Mabu Market and rushed to find a Water Viper attacking the timid Mabu who work there.

"No gold! No glory!"

Trigger Happy was the first Skylander to leap from the Portal of Power, which had transported the three heroes to Mabu Market. He was a giggling gremlin, covered in rust-colored fur and with a ridiculously long tongue that lolled out of his permanently grinning mouth.

But his tongue wasn't the first thing people usually noticed about Trigger Happy. No, the first thing was the two massive golden guns he held in his hands.

Trigger Happy was the best shot in Skylands. In fact, he still is. He never misses, but his guns don't fire bullets or missiles; his shiny shooters fire gold coins. This is why people cheer when Trigger Happy appears and sends bad guys packing. Not only does he rid your home town of wrongdoers, but he'll also leave so much gold ammo lying around that you'll be rich for the rest of your life.

Usually Trigger Happy likes to shoot first and answer questions later (most of the time he forgets to ask the questions at all). However, even he paused when he saw the state of Mabu Market.

What has halted Trigger Happy in his tracks? What has the Water Viper done to Mabu Market? And can Kaos be stopped from conquering Skylands?

Find out all of the answers in the unmissable final installment of the Mask of Power . . .

TRIGGER HAPPY
TARGETS THE EVIL KAOS

Also available:

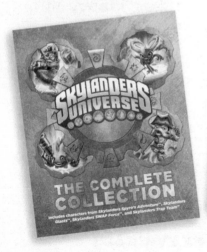